# The Christmas Garden

John Alexander

Copyright © 2014 John Alexander

All rights reserved.

ISBN:1502756099
ISBN-13:9781502756091

# DEDICATION

This story is dedicated to my grandchildren who inspire me.

# CONTENTS

ACKNOWLEDGMENTS ......................i

1 HAUNTED HOUSE .......................1

2 THE DREAM .............................6

3 BRAVERY ..................................8

4 FOREBODING...........................14

5 SPOTTED.................................17

6 EXPANSION .............................20

7 THE PREDICTION.....................23

8 DARKNESS...............................25

9 THE PLAN................................29

10 FACE TO FACE......................32

11 THE FROG .............................39

12 ORDINANCES ........................42

13 THE SEARCH .........................44

14 COOKIES ...............................47

15 GAINING SUPPORT ................51

16 THE NOTICE ..........................53

17 CONFRONTATION....................60

18 THE IDEA ..............................64

19 COUNCIL MEETING .................67

20 LIGHTS ..................................77

ABOUT THE AUTHOR....................80

## ACKNOWLEDGMENTS

I extend special thanks to my wife who supports me and encourages me to write and a big thank you to my daughter and grandchildren who provide insight and inspiration.

# 1 HAUNTED HOUSE

**My** third grade year? To tell you the truth, I like it in the middle. With some new kids in lower grades to boss around, an older sister in the fourth grade to blaze the trail, and the first two years of elementary school behind me, what more could I want? I have to admit my sister is still my best friend and I like having her around. For me I'll always remember this year as the year of the Christmas garden. Let me tell you why.

School got off to a normal start. Amber and I walked home together since all the elementary grade classes ended at the same time. Our walks home together began the day I entered first grade. We have taken various routes home over the years, but I decided we needed a change.

"Let's go home a different way today," I said.

"I'm game," Amber said. "After math class today, a girl told me about a spooky old house that is supposedly haunted. It's a few blocks over from our normal route home. Want to check it out?"

"Perfect. Let's do it," I replied. "You lead the way."

Amber slowed as the house came into sight. It stood at the end of a dead end street, and we could tell from the yard that this house appeared spooky. Grass, weeds, and undergrowth surrounded the house. I could see the second story, but not the first floor. The weeds and undergrowth blocked our view.

Amber stopped. "I'm not walking down there. This is close enough for me. Autumn, if you have any sense, you'll not go any closer either."

I did not say a word since I did not want Amber to hear any fear in my voice. I waved at her as I walked very slowly toward the end of the road. I stopped and took in the scene before me. The battered old mailbox sat crooked on the post. The old gate hung by two rusty hinges attached to an iron post and had seen its better days. The iron fence stood about five feet tall and arrows pointed skyward at the top. I scanned the windows on the top floor looking for any signs of life. I could make out thin white curtains on the inside of the windows. I fixed my gaze on one window where I thought I saw movement. I looked for several minutes and dismissed it as just my imagination. When I turned to leave, I'm certain that the curtain in that room moved.

"What did you see?" Amber asked when I got back to where she stood.

"It's spooky alright," I said. "I thought I saw movement on the second floor, but I'm not sure."

"You saw someone or something move?"

Amber asked. "I'm glad I stayed here. That's creepy."

We continued our walk home and talked about our day, but I couldn't get that old house out of my mind.

## 2 THE DREAM

**I** woke up with my head going from one side to the other. Straddling me with her knees Amber shook me back and forth.

"Autumn, wake up!" Amber said over and over.

"I'm awake now," I said. "What's going on? It's the middle of the night."

"You have to promise me you'll never go

near that house again," Amber said.

"And why not?" I asked.

"I had a dream," she said. "But not like any other one, ever. I saw you locked up in that house in a dark room. Then the door began to open and I felt your fear. I woke up before I saw whoever or whatever kept you captive in that room."

"It was just a bad dream," I said. "Go back to sleep, and next time keep me out of your nightmares."

"It's a sign, and you better take it seriously," she said. I heard the fear in her voice.

## 3 BRAVERY

**Toward** the end of the following week, the days grew cooler. I always loved the first chilly days of fall. Crisp air invigorated me as Amber and I began our walk home from school.

"I'm going by the old house today," I announced. "You coming with me?"

"No way," Amber said. "I don't want you

THE CHRISTMAS GARDEN

near that place either. Remember my dream?"

"I remember, but I don't want to go straight home today," I said. "I enjoy the cool fall air, and I'm going, with or without you."

"Suit yourself," she said. "Dig your own grave. I'll have no part of it."

Amber left walking swiftly toward home and I proceeded down the street with the house at the end of it. I stood once again at the gate looking for signs of life. The squirrels scurried about in the big oak tree in the front yard. The leaves showed off their orange brilliance.

After several minutes I gathered my courage and moved the latch on the gate and pulled it toward me very slowly. The gate creaked loudly as I eased it open just enough to slide inside. I could see some trampled grass, which formed a narrow winding trail. I slowly took one step at a time trying to not make a sound. Twigs crunched under my feet as I walked and made more noise than I wanted. I paused between each step listening for any movement coming from the direction of the house. After what seemed like an eternity, I reached a spot where I could see the outline of the porch railing and the top of the front door.

I stood frozen trying to decide if I should go any further. Suddenly I heard the gate open behind me, and someone walking quickly in my direction. I ran to my right and buried myself in the tall grass. I could now see the porch and stay out of sight at the same time. My heart pounded as the footsteps came up the path beside me and then continued past me. I saw a man walk up the steps onto the porch and place two full grocery sacks on the wooden porch. He lifted the lid on an urn, took out some bills, and put change back into the urn and replaced the lid. He stood for a few minutes looking at the remains of a yard. His gaze went back and forth across my hiding place. I remained motionless except for the rapid beating of my heart. At last he went back down the steps and beyond me on the path. I heard the gate creak as he left.

I waited motionless with my eyes fixed on the grocery bags on the porch. Several minutes passed and I thought my wait might last longer than I could be still. Just as I started to change positions, the inside door opened slowly and I saw a figure on the other side of the screen door.

The dusty grass tickled my nose. "I will not sneeze," I told myself.

The screen door opened slowly and a woman dressed in a long dark dress used a cane as she walked to the urn, removed the remaining money, and slipped it into her pocket. She picked up the bags with one hand and held the cane with her other hand. I heard the tapping of the cane stop as she turned and surveyed the yard, cocking her head to one side as though listening for the slightest movement. Her eyes stopped briefly on the spot I occupied and then moved past me. She went back into the house and I finally exhaled. My felt my

THE CHRISTMAS GARDEN

heart pounding in my neck as though it lodged itself in my throat.

I crept slowly out of my nest and took precise, methodical steps up the narrow path, staying ducked down as low as I could. I reached the gate and luckily the man left it ajar just enough for me to squeeze through without a sound. I looked over my shoulder and saw a curtain pulled back to the side in the same second story window I remembered from my first visit. As I stared at the window the curtain dropped and covered the window. I ran as fast as I could and stopped at the end of the block to catch my breath.

## 4 FOREBODING

**"Well**, did you go or did you chicken out?"
Amber asked.

"Yes, I did go," I answered.

"Anything change from last week?" she
asked.

"I slipped inside the gate this time," I
said.

"You went in that jungle of a yard?"

Amber asked.

"I had to hide when a man came in the yard and delivered two grocery bags to the front porch," I said. Amber's eyes opened wide at this point. "I waited after he was gone and saw a woman dressed in dark clothes carrying a cane get the groceries. I looked back from the gate when I left and I think she saw me."

"How do you know she saw you?" Amber asked, eyes still wide open.

"I saw a curtain pulled back in the upstairs window, and it closed while I was looking straight at the window," I said.

"Your goose is so cooked," Amber said. "I just know she's a witch, and you probably already have a curse on you just for trespassing."

"And how did you come to that conclusion?" I asked.

"Are you kidding?" she said. "Long dark clothes, a cane, old house with grass taller than us. What more do you want? I can feel those beady eyes staring at you from the window. That creeps me out."

"I was plenty scared," I said. "My heart beat ninety miles an hour, but I'm not convinced she's a witch just based on clothes, a cane, and an over grown yard. I need to know more."

"You're not going back there ever again are you?" Amber asked.

"We'll see," I said. "We'll see."

# 5 SPOTTED

**The** rest of the week I could not get the old woman off my mind. I asked others in my class, and everyone said the pretty much the same thing. "I had no idea someone lived there, but if someone lives there, she certainly wants to be left alone. She may also be a witch and would not hesitate to use her powers on anyone who intrudes on her property. You were lucky to get away without her seeing you."

I made up my mind. Today I would go by that house on the way home and at least stand outside the gate and look for any movement inside the house.

The tall growth in the yard hid my walk to the gate, so I felt fairly secure as I crept along the fence. The top of the closed gate loomed above my head. Between the iron tips at the top, I could clearly see the second floor windows. A gentle breeze blew the curtains exposed by an opened window in the center of the house. The curtains parted and I clearly saw a woman standing in the window. Her silver laced black hair played across her face as the breeze teased it back and forth. Her gaze locked on the

THE CHRISTMAS GARDEN

gate and she leaned forward on the windowsill.

I froze. I could feel her eyes penetrating into my mind. I wanted to run, but I could not pull myself from her stare. The window slammed shut. I thought I could hear the sound of footsteps descending the stairs inside the house. Now free of her gaze and fully alert, I ran as fast as I could and didn't stop until I reached my own front porch. I stood there for several minutes catching my breath before I went inside.

# 6 EXPANSION

**"Thanks** for suggesting we meet here, Ron," John said as he sat down at the table. "I like this little coffee house."

"Yes, it's a nice quiet place for a conversation," Ron said. "This little nook on the square brings back lots of memories."

"I bet it does," John said. "This place used to be a drug store years ago, right?"

"Yes, it was quite the hang out during high school," Ron said. "The old soda fountain had a marble top and must have been at least twenty feet long. The round stools were attached to the tile floor."

John paused and sipped has coffee. "I wanted to discuss some ideas I have about the future growth of this town," John said.

"What kind of ideas?" Ron asked. "The town has been growing nicely, especially since the downtown renovation began last year."

"Exactly," John said. "The revitalization of this downtown area is drawing more people and the retailers are seeing more revenue. I want to make sure that continues and that there's room for expansion."

"What do you have in mind?" Ron asked.

"I think we need to relocate the park at the northeast corner of the square," John said. "That park covers over five acres of prime real estate that could be used by future businesses."

"John, this town needs a park," Ron said. "The park has been on that spot since before I was born."

"I agree we need a park near the downtown area," John said. "But I'd rather see that land used for commerce. We can find another location for a park. If the city sells the land, we'll have more than enough for a nice new park nearby."

"I'll have to get used to the idea," Ron said. "Let me think about it. I think it will be hard to get approved."

# 7 THE PREDICTION

**No** matter how hard I tried, I could not get that woman out of my head. What happened to her? Why did she live all closed off from the outside world? Did she ever get out? I need a new tactic, but what else can I do?

Amber walked into the room. "What's on your mind? You have that far off look on your face."

"I'm still thinking about that woman in the old house with the jungle in the front yard," I answered.

"I thought you dropped that weeks ago," Amber said.

"I have gone by there a few more times since then," I said.

"She's going to put a spell on you," Amber said. "Don't say I didn't warn you when she turns you into something dreadful."

"So you still think she's a witch?" I asked.

"You bet I do," Amber said. "Why else would she live like that?"

"I don't know," I said. "I really don't know."

# 8 DARKNESS

**The** sun had set and only a few minutes of daylight remained.

"Mom, I need to return a book I borrowed. Do you mind if I ride my bike to Jennifer's house and return it?" I asked.

"It's almost dark," Mom said. "Stay on the sidewalk and walk your bike when you cross streets. I hate to have you out on your bike at night. Come straight home when you're done."

"Will do. Thanks Mom," I said as I walked out the front door and grabbed my bike.

By the time I had dropped off the book at Jennifer's house darkness engulfed the neighborhood around me. When I reached the street with the jungle yard house, I decided to take a quick detour and see it at night. I rode slowly up the sidewalk to the gate and made certain my bike made no sound. No lights showed up in any of the windows. I stood still for several minutes looking intently for any sign of movement on the second floor.

I heard a creak and I swallowed hard trying to slow my heart rate. I heard it again, and then a third time. I realized the sound came from the front porch. Creak, creak, I perceived the back and forth motion of a porch swing and I stood mesmerized.

The sound stopped and the swing jerked as someone got up. Footsteps sounded on the porch, then nothing. Did she see me? I took off on my bike and peddled as fast as I could. My house never looked so good as I rounded the final turn. I waited a few minutes for my breathing to return to normal before going back into the house.

Amber's words haunted me as witches and curses dominated my dreams. I looked hard in the bathroom mirror several times the next morning to make sure the curses only took place in my dreams and did not carry over into real life. Fortunately I saw no changes.

## 9 THE PLAN

**Weeks** passed and I managed to stay away from that house, but it still haunted my dreams and thoughts. Why the incessant focus on the house and the person who lived there? Did she put a spell on me after all? With Halloween only a few days away, I made up my mind to confront my fears.

If I saw any sign of light on Halloween

night, I planned to walk onto that porch, knock on her door and pay her a trick or treat visit. A lump formed in my throat just thinking about it. Hopefully Amber would join me, but even if she chickened out, I had made up my mind to do it, one way or another.

Amber met me as I walked out of my last class for the day. We walked in silence for a few minutes, and then Amber asked, "What are you wearing for Halloween this year?"

"I don't know for sure. I've decided to knock on the door of the jungle yard house Halloween night," I said.

"You can't be serious," Amber said.

"What better excuse to knock on someone's door? What do you think I should

THE CHRISTMAS GARDEN

wear in case she does come to the door dressed as a witch?" I asked.

"I think you're nuts. Don't expect me to go with you. I have no clue what you should wear, but please wear tennis shoes in case you need to make a fast get away. I'm not setting foot on that porch," Amber said.

"Will you at least watch from the gate as my backup?" I asked. "Please."

"I'll think about it, but I'm making no promises," Amber said.

"Thanks for at least considering it," I said.

## 10 FACE TO FACE

I stood at the gate wearing an angel costume. I turned to Amber and said, "I'm not sure I can do it."

"You've come this far," Amber said. "You can't back out now."

"My mouth is so dry I think my tongue could crack open," I said.

Amber pulled a small bottle of water out

THE CHRISTMAS GARDEN

of her purse. "Here, have a swig and relax. Remember, you're the brave one who's always the first to try any new rides at the park every year. This can't be as bad as that. What's the worst thing that could ... Don't answer that."

"If she turns me into a frog, you promise to take me home and take care of me?" I asked.

"I'll make sure you get plenty of food and water," Amber said. "What do frogs eat anyway?"

"Flies and other small insects," I said.

"Yuck," Amber said. "Make sure you don't stare into her eyes. I expect you back soon, so don't hang around long."

I tried to open the gate as quietly as possible, but it made a terrible squeaking noise, even worse than I remembered. I waited for movement and heard nothing. I put one foot into the tall grass, then another. My heart pounded faster with each step as though my heart made up for the slow movement of my feet. Pausing frequently, I listened for any sounds in the yard or beyond. I stood rigid when crickets suddenly bust into song in the crisp night air. The chill that went up my spine slowly subsided and I continued my approach.

The clouds covered the moon and shut off any light. I could just make out the outline of the house and as I got nearer, I could see the edge of the porch. I put my foot on the first step and made my way up in almost complete darkness. I saw a faint light through one of the windows as I walked

## THE CHRISTMAS GARDEN

slowly toward the door.

"My, aren't you the brave one," came from my right.

Startled, confused, and frightened I just froze. "What do I do now?" I thought to myself. I'm on the porch and now she's seen me. With no clue what to say I blurted out, "Are you the lady of the house?"

"Yes, this is my house. What brings you here?" she said. Her voice crackled at bit.

"It's Halloween and I've come to trick or treat," I said trying not to sound scared.

"Come here so I can get a look at you," she said.

I walked in the direction of the sound and got close enough to make out the form of a woman seated in a swing.

"Come sit down," she said patting the

space beside her on the swing.

"If it's ok with you, I'd rather stand," I said.

"I won't bite," she said. "Or do you believe the gossip that I'm a witch?"

"I don't know what to believe, but I wanted to find out for myself rather than just accept gossip," I said.

"Good for you," she said. "It's always best to check things out for yourself. What's your name?"

"My name is Autumn. What's your name?"

"Pleased to meet you Autumn," she said. "My name is Abigail Murray. You can call me Ms. Abbey. Now that we're properly introduced, come sit with me on the swing. My hearing is not as good as it used to be."

## THE CHRISTMAS GARDEN

I walked to Ms. Abbey and sat down as far away as possible on that porch swing. "Ms. Abbey, do you practice magic?" I asked. "Please don't put a spell on me."

Ms. Abbey's laughter filled the night air. "Baby girl, I can assure you I know no magic. If I could perform magic, I'd have this place looking immaculate."

"How did the yard get so grown up and out of control?" I asked.

"My husband loved to garden," she said. "He planted beautiful shrubs, trees, and flowers. This six-acre plot of ground resembled a well-manicured English garden. When he died, I could not keep it up. My arthritis prevents me from getting around very well. I live on a very limited income from social security and I can't afford to hire it done."

"I'm sorry you lost your husband," I said. "Can your children help?"

"We had no children," she said. "We were both only children with no brothers or sisters. We always wanted a family, but it just never happened."

"I'm sorry you have no family," I said.

## 11 THE FROG

**The** frog croaked and jumped right between Amber's feet. Amber's mouth dropped open and she stepped back in disbelief. "Autumn, is that you," she said in a hushed tone. The frog croaked again. Amber grabbed the frog and carefully placed it in her trick or treat bag and ran home as fast as her legs could carry her. She stopped at the front porch to catch her breath.

She carefully opened the sack and peered inside. The frog's sides rhythmically expanded and contracted. Amber walked up the stairs contemplating what to do next. She went into the bedroom she shared with Autumn, retrieved a shoebox from the shelf and dumped out the shoes. She punched holes in the lid, carefully placed the frog in the box, and shut the lid.

Sleep overcame her soon after she lay down on the bed with the box held against her side. Startled awake by a noise, she looked at the box and held it up in front of her.

"Autumn, can you hear me?" Amber asked.

"Yes, of course I can hear you," came

the reply.

Amber stared at the box in disbelief.

"I'm listening. What's up?" I said as I opened the door. I saw Amber sitting on the bed. All the blood left her face leaving her as white as a sheet. "You look like you've just seen a ghost," I said. "What's wrong? Is Mom ok?"

Amber had trouble getting words out of her mouth. Finally she managed to utter, "I thought she turned you in to a frog." Holding up the box she added, "This frog."

I tried to choke back my laugh, but I just couldn't hold it. I laughed first. Then Amber managed to giggle a bit, then we both laughed and rolled on the bed until tears ran down our cheeks. "Let's go free a frog," I said and we laughed even more.

# 12 ORDINANCES

**Books** surrounded John on the table in the back corner of the library. For the last week and a half he had spent at least an hour each afternoon in the legal reference section of the library. His current text contained city ordinances dating back to the late 1800s when the town first incorporated.

He occasionally chuckled at some of the

laws still on the books. The early city fathers especially frowned on spitting. They spelled out illegal spitting practices in great detail including where, when, and under what circumstances one could not legally expel liquids from the mouth. John pulled himself away from the rather lengthy saliva ordinances and continued his legal investigation.

He searched through two volumes of city ordinances. "The city must surely have an ordinance to seize property," he mumbled as he thumbed through the pages.

# 13 THE SEARCH

**Ron** drove through the streets within six blocks of the downtown area. Harley, his golden retriever, sat in his usual spot in the passenger seat looking out the window. Ron carried on conversations with Harley during their drives around town. Most of the town's folks knew Harley by name and offered him treats whenever possible. Harley had grown to expect pats and goodies and thoroughly enjoyed his adoring fans.

"Not much vacant land near town Harley," Ron said.

Harley looked at Ron as though acknowledging his agreement.

"The few lots that are vacant are way too small for a park," Ron continued. "I think John's park relocation plans may not get off the ground."

Harley yawned.

Ron laughed. "My sentiments exactly. I'm not crazy about his idea either."

Ron continued meandering through the streets and alleys near downtown, expanding his search in a large spiral. "Many of the homesteads sit on large lots with multiple acres big enough for a park, but buying a homestead just to get the land would be very expensive."

Harley looked at Ron as he spoke and then returned his attention to the window to make sure he didn't miss anything.

## 14 COOKIES

**Amber** and I opened the gate and scurried to Ms. Abbey's porch for the third time during the last few weeks.

"Good afternoon girls," Ms. Abbey said. "Come sit in the swing while I get the cookies I baked. I just took them out of the oven. They'll be good and hot."

Amber gave me the look.

"What?" I asked.

"Have you ever eaten anything here?" Amber asked.

"Amber, you need to get a grip," I said. "She's not a witch, she doesn't make poison cookies, and she doesn't eat children. She's just a widow lady who's lived a long time, and due to health issues she doesn't get out much any more."

"Yeah, you're probably right as usual," Amber said.

Ms. Abbey returned with a basket of cookies in one hand and her cane in the other. "Eat one while they're still warm."

I took one bite and noticed Amber waited until I swallowed to take a bite. "This cookie is amazing," I said.

"I'm glad you like them," Ms. Abbey said.

THE CHRISTMAS GARDEN

"Would you mind coming in the house to help me bring out some glasses and some lemonade?"

"I'll help," we both said at once.

"Thank you. You can both help," Ms. Abbey said.

I walked in first followed by Amber and Ms. Abbey. After my eyes adjusted to the dark room I stepped back in time. The wallpaper, the furniture, and the floors resembled what I would see in a museum. I walked toward the dim light coming from the kitchen. I tried not to stare.

"I guess you're surprised by the furniture," Ms. Abbey said.

"Yes, it is very old," Amber said.

"My late husband loved antique furniture," Ms. Abbey said. "Most of what I have in the house belonged to his family, passed down through many generations. It's a bit old for my taste, but I couldn't part with it since his family line ended when he died."

"What will become of it after you're gone?" I asked.

"He stipulated in his will that it would be mine for the rest of my life and then would go to a museum for others to enjoy and remember the past," Ms. Abbey answered.

We visited with Ms. Abbey for almost an hour. "We need to go start on our homework," I said.

"We enjoyed the visit," Amber said.

"Come back soon," Ms. Abbey said as she waved goodbye.

## 15 GAINING SUPPORT

**"I'm** surprised the council members supported your idea to move the park so easily," Ron said.

"I've been working behind the scenes," John said. "It wasn't easy, but I did manage to gain their support one by one over the last few weeks."

"I spent time investigating all the

potential sites within six blocks of the downtown square," Ron said. "I did not find a single location suitable for the park."

"Don't waste any more time looking for a location," John said. "Just leave that in my capable hands. I have some ideas."

"Works for me," Ron said. "Let me know if you change your mind. I'll be glad to help."

# 16 THE NOTICE

**I** don't know if the teachers intentionally planned it but by the end of the week following Halloween every single teacher gave us large projects due the second week of November so they could grade them before Thanksgiving. I spent my afternoons getting a head start on all of the projects.

Time at the library and time at home

left no opportunity to visit with Ms. Abbey for two full weeks. Although I'd only visited with her a few times right after Halloween, I missed our visits.

"Amber, I'm stopping by to see Ms. Abbey this afternoon. Do you want to join me?" I asked.

"Sorry, I'm going to a friend's house this afternoon. You sure you'll be all right by yourself?" she asked.

"I'll be fine. Not to worry," I said.

"See you later," Amber said as she continued down the sidewalk.

"See ya," I said and waved as I turned down the dead end street towards Ms. Abbey's place. The growth surrounding the house, now brown with only a little green showing through, seemed thicker and more

THE CHRISTMAS GARDEN

foreboding.

As I made my way to the porch, the stems and branches pulled at my jeans and shirt. The steps creaked as I ascended and planks on the porch echoed my approach. I raised my hand to knock but the inside door opened before my knuckles reached the wood.

"Hello Autumn," Ms. Abbey said. "I'm glad you stopped by. Did you smell my pies on your way home?"

"No Mam, but I do smell them now," I said.

"Come in and sit down," she said as we walked back to the kitchen at the rear of the house. I sat down at the kitchen table and Ms. Abbey cut a piece of pie for each of us and brought them to the table, one small plate and napkin at a time. "Dive in while it's hot," she said as she pointed to my plate.

I didn't hesitate to take a bite. "Sorry it's been a while," I said. "The teachers decided to pile on homework projects all at the same time," I said.

"Do you have them all done yet?" she asked.

"No, but I have started all of them and know what I need to do to finish," I said.

"Good for you," she said. "I always liked to get started early."

We ate in silence for a few minutes. "How are you doing?" I asked after devouring the pie.

"I'm a bit down today," she said. "I baked pies to take my mind off of it."

"What happened?" I asked.

"I received an eviction notice from the city this morning," she said. "They quoted some nonsense about property upkeep ordinances and their ability to take possession of my homestead."

"They can't do that," I said.

"They plan to discuss it at the city council meeting next week," she said.

"Is the meeting closed, or is it open to the public?" I asked.

"The notice said it's a public meeting," she said.

I put my plate and fork in the sink, thanked Ms. Abbey, excused myself, and got home as quickly as I could. How could the city evict an elderly widow from her home?

"Mom, are you home?" I called as I closed the front door.

"I'm in the kitchen," she said.

I sat down on a bar stool still breathing hard from my fast walk home. "Do you know anyone on the city council?" I asked.

"Well, Ron who lives down the street is on the city council," she said. "Why do you ask?"

"I just want to find out about the upcoming city council meeting agenda," I said. "I heard they plan to evict a widow from her home and I want to find out if it's true."

"Surely not," she said. "Get on the computer and find the city web site. The site lists the council members and their phone numbers. You can probably catch him at home this time of day."

I spoke with Ron and told him what I

had learned. He said he'd check into the matter and let me know what he found out. He agreed that the city, even if the ordinance existed, should not take away someone's home, especially a widow.

## 17 CONFRONTATION

**Ron** sat down in the secluded booth in the corner of the café. The waitress appeared within minutes. "Want some coffee?" she asked carrying a cup and a coffee pot on a tray. "I just made a fresh pot."

"Yes, coffee would be great," Ron said.

"Want to order yet, or will someone else be joining you?" she asked.

## THE CHRISTMAS GARDEN

"I'll wait to order. John should be here in a few minutes," Ron answered.

"I'll show him back when he arrives," she said. She gave Ron his coffee and left to make sure her other guests had full cups.

John soon arrived with the waitress right behind him. "Coffee?" she asked. John nodded and she gave him a full cup and darted back toward the kitchen.

"You come here often?" John asked as he sipped his coffee.

"Guilty," Ron answered. "The coffee is hot and my cup is never empty."

"Will you be able to make the council meeting next week?" John asked.

"I'll be there," Ron said. "What's on the agenda so far?"

"I have found a solution to the park

location," John said. "I'll put forth the recommendation in the meeting."

"What is your solution?" Ron asked.

"There's an overgrown mess of a property that a woman currently occupies," John said. "Legally we can force her out of the property and take possession of it, but I hope it doesn't come to that. The place is obviously more than she can maintain and she needs to find somewhere else to live."

"You plan to force an old woman out of her home so you can move the park?" Ron asked. "You really think the city council will even consider evicting an old woman?"

"I wouldn't put it like that," John said. "It's more like we're enabling a widow to move to more suitable housing and assisting her with the process without the hassle of trying to sell her existing property. It's a win-win situation."

"Good luck with that," Ron said. "I don't see any upside for the widow who's kicked out of her home."

"She's got no family and should be in a retirement home," John said. "The one in town will provide room and board for less than the average social security payment. She'll be fine."

"She'll lose her independence and her quality of life," Ron said.

"We'll just have to agree to disagree on that point," John said. "Think about it before the council meeting. It's for her own good and also for the good of the town."

# 18 THE IDEA

**I** visited Ms. Abbey every single day leading

up to the council meeting. Amber joined me

most days. We all shared ideas regarding

her next course of action but nothing

helped.

The night before the council meeting

day, Amber and I reviewed all the possible

ways we had discussed with Ms. Abbey to

either find a new place or prevent the city from taking her property.

"I don't see any way to solve Ms. Abbey's dilemma, either to find a new place that meets her needs or to stop the city from relocating the park," Amber said.

"Perhaps we've not considered all the options," I said. "What if we find a way to keep Ms. Abbey in her home and move the park?"

"What do you propose?" Amber asked. "We can't have Ms. Abbey and the park there."

"Why not?" I asked.

"You mean have Ms. Abbey living in the park like a homeless person?" Amber asked.

"What if the city had the park on the land Ms. Abbey owns and Ms. Abbey keeps her house?" I suggested.

The next afternoon, we arrived at Ms. Abbey's house eager to discuss our proposal. Ms. Abbey listened intently as we described our idea. She asked a lot of questions, but in the end she hugged us both and called us brilliant.

## 19 COUNCIL MEETING

**That** night Amber and I assisted Ms. Abbey, Amber on one side and me on the other. We walked into the large meeting hall packed with people. Word traveled quickly in a small town, and many knew the agenda included the house occupied by the old woman. I stayed out of the way of her cane so she could make her way down the steps of the center isle to the front row. The room became eerily silent as attendees noticed her presence. I could hear whispers behind us as we passed.

We sat through the mundane business that seemed to take forever. First the secretary read the minutes from the last meeting and members nit picked small details until finally approving the minutes. The secretary then read the agenda and opened the floor for other recommendations for items to be considered. No one added to the agenda, but the council's approval of the agenda moved at a snail's pace. This first city council meeting of my life did not motivate me to run for office anytime soon.

While working slowly through all the other agenda items, the room remained

THE CHRISTMAS GARDEN

packed awaiting the one item that drew the large crowd to the meeting. Finally the secretary read aloud the proposal to relocate the park. Everyone remained quiet and still. She ended by asking, "Does anyone wish to address the council regarding this matter?"

More than a dozen people lined up along the center isle to wait for a turn at the microphone.

The secretary addressed the line of speakers. "You will each have three minutes. Use the time wisely and respectfully. The first person in line may step to the microphone and begin."

The array of speakers reflected the complexity of the proposal, expressing outright disgust at the thought of taking away a widow's home, as well as support for downtown growth. An equal number of speakers addressed both sides of the issue. After a long thirty minutes, the last speaker had his say and sat down.

"Does anyone else have anything to say?" the secretary asked.

Ms. Abbey stood and walked with her cane to the podium. "I'm Abigail Murray and I own the property under discussion. May I speak?"

"Yes, Mrs. Murray, you may have as much time as you need," the secretary said.

"I have lived in this town longer than most anyone here, and before most of the esteemed council members were born." Ms. Abbey paused as a hushed laughter rippled through the crowd. Ms. Abbey continued.

THE CHRISTMAS GARDEN

"I'm not able to get out and about much any more, but I am proud of the growth in the community these last few years, and the revitalization of the downtown that I've seen reported on the local news. This town is growing again and a lot of new families will keep it growing." Ms. Abbey paused to catch her breath and switched gears.

"When I received the eviction notice several weeks ago a deep sadness overcame me. My life seemed pretty useless and hopeless. I had no idea what I would do. I don't have much, but I at least have my home. The idea of losing the place my late husband and I made our home for decades devastated me. What would I do without my home full of memories?" Ms. Abbey paused and wiped a tear with her handkerchief. I saw several others around the room do the same.

"I recently made two new friends who helped me deal with this possibility," she said. "Autumn and Amber," she said to us, "Please stand up so everyone can see you."

I stood up and Amber joined me as we turned to view the packed rows of people behind us. I saw Mom on the isle several rows back and waved. The people politely applauded and we quickly sat back down.

"These girls are wise beyond their years," Ms. Abbey said. "They came up with an idea which I think is wonderful. First let me give you some background. I have little money but my social security checks meet my basic needs. I am a widow. My husband died many years ago. Neither of us had

## THE CHRISTMAS GARDEN

brothers or sisters. I'm the end of the line with no next of kin." Ms. Abbey again paused to catch her breath.

"Here's the proposal to the council," Ms. Abbey said. "I will deed my land and my home to the city with one stipulation. I can live in my home for as long as I live. The land can be transformed into a park for everyone to enjoy, and I can live out my life in my home, and enjoy the sounds of fun and laughter surrounding me."

The crowd stood to their feet and applauded, whistled, and shouted words of agreement. The council members immediately huddled for several minutes.

"We unanimously accept to your offer," John said. "We will meet with our legal team in the morning and get the ball rolling."

A gentleman to my left and about half way back walked from his seat to the microphone. "Mrs. Murray, you may not remember me," he said. "My landscaping company maintained your place for several years before your husband died. It would be my honor to remove the dead grass, weeds, and shrubs from your yard and replace them with new plants and add new sod in your front and back yard. That way you'll have a small fenced in yard for some privacy."

Ms. Abbey gave him a big hug. "Thank you son. You are very generous."

The gentleman addressed the council. "That covers about half an acre of the six acre homestead. If you need more landscape material, I will provide it to the city at cost. The park means a lot to me and my family."

"Let the record show that we accept his generous offer," John said.

"It is duly recorded," the secretary said.

"If anyone else wants to donate time or materials please contact one of the council members," Ron said. "Thank you all for your participation and generosity. The community stood together tonight inspired by two special girls. Amber and Autumn, please stand up once again."

We stood up a second time and turned around. The crowd erupted in applause this time. They stood, they stomped their feet, and they shouted.

"Way to go ... great idea ... you'll go far in life ... born leaders ..."

When the eruption subsided I took my

seat, still blushing. Amber looked at me, grinned, and shrugged her shoulders. We weren't accustomed to that much attention. I looked back at Mom and I could see her pride as she smiled at us.

# 20 LIGHTS

**By** the first week of December, the time, energy, and generosity of many people transformed Ms. Abbey's homestead into a beautiful garden. The council members invited everyone to attend the annual Christmas tree lighting ceremony in the new park.

On the night of the big event, Ms. Abbey

stepped up to the ceremonial switch to officially light the giant tree. John approached the microphone to begin the ceremony.

"Ladies and gentlemen and children of all ages, I bid you welcome. This transformation reflects what we have accomplished in our town. It represents hope, generosity, and good will, both now and for future generations. It gives me great pleasure, before we light the tree, to unveil the park entrance."

The cover over the park entrance archway dropped to the ground revealing a large beautiful wrought iron crescent with ABBEY PARK embossed in the center surrounded by roses.

"Mrs. Abigail Murray, you will be

## THE CHRISTMAS GARDEN

remembered forever for your generous gift to this town. May you enjoy your life in this lush setting for the rest of your life. You may now light the tree."

Ms. Abbey pulled the lever and the tree lights glowed with a gorgeous array of colors. Seconds later other lights throughout the park glistened. Amber and I stood in amazement at all the lights. Ms. Abbey turned to us and said, "Thanks to the two of you, instead of living in a jungle full of thorns, now I live in a Christmas garden."

# ABOUT THE AUTHOR

During the last five years of his forty-four year career in the high tech industry John discovered his love for writing. He now spends full time pursuing that passion. The books in the Amber-Autumn mystery series celebrate not only his grandchildren but children everywhere. They will lead the future.